CAMP TIGER

G. P. PUTNAM'S SONS, an imprint of Penguin Random House LLC, New York ⓟ Text copyright © 2019 by Susan Choi. Illustrations copyright © 2019 by John Rocco. Penguin supports copyright. Copyright fuels creativity, encourages diverse voices, promotes free speech, and creates a vibrant culture. Thank you for buying an authorized edition of this book and for complying with copyright laws by not reproducing, scanning, or distributing any part of it in any form without permission. You are supporting writers and allowing Penguin to continue to publish books for every reader. • G. P. Putnam's Sons is a registered trademark of Penguin Random House LLC. • Library of Congress Cataloging-in-Publication Data | Names: Choi, Susan, 1969– author. | Rocco, John, illustrator. | Title: Camp tiger / Susan Choi ; illustrated by John Rocco. Description: New York, NY : G. P. Putnam's Sons, [2019] Summary: A talking tiger approaches a family during their annual end-of-summer camping trip and is befriended by the youngest, a boy who does not feel ready for first grade. | Identifiers: LCCN 2017061064 | ISBN 9780399173295 (hardcover) | ISBN 9780525516705 (ebook) Subjects: | CYAC: Camping—Fiction. | Tiger—Fiction. | Family life—Fiction. Classification: LCC PZ7.1.C533 Cam 2019 | DDC [E]—dc23 | LC record available at https://lccn.loc.gov/2017061064 • Manufactured in China by RR Donnelley Asia Printing Solutions Ltd. • ISBN 9780399173295 • 10 9 8 7 6 5 4 3 2 1 • Design by Jaclyn Reyes and Dave Kopka. Text set in Weiss. The artwork in this book was created using a watercolor sketch and wash pencil and then adding the color digitally.

CAMP TIGER

written by SUSAN CHOI

illustrated by JOHN ROCCO

putnam

G. P. PUTNAM'S SONS

Every year, my mom and dad and brother and I go camping at Mountain Pond. We drive a long time on the highway, and then a long time on roads that zigzag, until we're on a road that's just dirt and rocks. The pine trees scrape the sides of our car. I think we're lost, and then the road zags and there's Mountain Pond, like a mirror in the trees.

It's September, the end of the summer. As soon as we get back from camping, we go back to school. My brother's starting fourth grade, and I'm starting first grade. I don't want to be a first grader. I liked kindergarten. I like Choice Time and building with blocks. I hope our camping trip never ends.

We have a campsite on the far side of the pond, with the big mountain starting behind it. My parents both really like it. "It's so beautiful," they say. "And so quiet."

We take our stuff out of the car and talk about all the things we'll see. The eagle fishing for its dinner in the pond. The salamander with red spots on its back. And the chipmunks that come to steal food while we sit by our campfire.

The air feels cool.
I find a red leaf on the ground.

While we're working on the tent, everything gets really still. My mom puts out her hand in that way that means *don't move* and *don't talk*.

A tiger steps silently out of the woods and stands next to the stone fireplace. The tiger is orange with black stripes and has a stern face and big, heavy paws. But it seems smaller than a tiger should be. It's still big—like our neighbor's German shepherd that scares me sometimes on the sidewalk— but for a tiger, it's small. It doesn't scare me. It also looks thin. And it talks.

"Do you have an extra tent?"
asks the tiger. "I have a cave,
but I still feel cold."

I know that we do. It's a two-person tent that we brought as a place for me and my brother to play if it rains.

"Yes," my dad finally says while my mom stares at him. "We'll set it up when we finish this one."

We set up the two tents in silence. I notice that, while we're working, the tiger starts acting like a cat—a more regular cat. He sits down and grooms himself slowly, especially cleaning his paws. I don't see claws. He must have them pulled in. I think he's cleaning himself to make us feel more comfortable with him. It works. My mom keeps looking over at him, and I can tell that she thinks he's beautiful.

When we're done, my dad holds out his arm in that goofy way of his that means *voila*!

"Can you unzip it for me?" the tiger asks.
I look at his huge, heavy paws.

My dad does, and the tiger lowers his
head and steps in carefully. I follow before
my parents can stop me.

"Zip us in, please," I call back.

"You can zip it yourself," my mom says. "Don't snag the fabric."

All summer, things my mom used to do for me—like make my bed in the morning or fold up my clothes—have become things that I have to do myself. I can do them, but I wish she would do them. This time, though, I zip the tent quickly, before she can make me come out.

Inside the tent, the tiger lies down so he's shaped like a C and puts his head on his paws. I wrap my arms around him and bury my face in his fur. He smells like sunshine and pine needles.

"Tigers live in Africa," I tell him.
"Not Africa. Asia," he says.
"This isn't Africa or Asia," I tell him.
"No," sighs the tiger.

All weekend, the tiger stays with us. When we hike on the trail, he walks first, and his paws make no sound. He knows an overlook we'd never found before, where we can see the tops of the green mountains stretching away.

He's cautious around water, but he comes with us in our canoe. He sits very still, staring out at the shore. I barely have to reach down to trail my hand in the water.

"The canoe's riding low," my dad says.

"Because of the weight of the tiger," I guess.

We paddle slowly so we won't tip over.

"You've grown, too," my mom says.

At the fishing spot, my brother catches
a pumpkinseed fish right away, which is what
always happens. "I don't want to fish," I say,
sitting next to the tiger. No one makes me.

But after a while, I get up and put bait on my hook. "I hate fish," I say as I cast.

"I love fish," says the tiger. "I'll eat any fish that you catch."

"I almost never catch any," I tell him. But today, I catch one.

"Just big enough to keep," says my dad when he measures.

"I'll eat it raw," says the tiger. "I like to eat the whole thing and feel its tail swish around in my stomach."

"Ugh!" we all say, but we're laughing.

We never see other people.
My mom says it's because it's
late in the season. Even the
park ranger never comes by.

Our last night, my brother and I get
to stay up extra late in the camp chairs
and watch the fire until it dies out. I can
see the tiger's eyes in the darkness, like
the very last embers. "I want to look for
shooting stars," I say. "I want to go in
the canoe, in the dark, and look up at the
stars." No one seems to hear but the tiger.

"I'll take you," he says.

The tiger pushes his paws through the sparkling black water instead of using a paddle. I steer, which I was never good at, except now I steer really well. I see the stars shining deep in the water, and our canoe gliding high in the sky. And then we're back, and my mom and dad lift me into our tent, not the tiger's, but I'm too tired to stop them.

The next morning, the tiger is gone. "He didn't say goodbye," I say. It's windy and cold, and that makes my eyes run and my throat feel thick, like I have a lump there. When my mom tries to give me oatmeal, I push it away.

"It's a wild animal," my dad says. "It had to go back where it came from."

"You can go say goodbye to the lake," says my mom.

I sit down by the water and put my head on my knees so my kneecaps press against my eyeballs. I hear my brother coming over to make fun of me, but instead, he just sits down nearby. Neither one of us says anything.

Leaves fly off the trees as we drive
back down out of the mountains.
"It's fall," says my mom.
   "That means it'll be cold," I say.
I think of the tiger shivering in
his cave.

When we get home that night, I draw the tiger exactly the way he looked. I'm going to take it to show my new teacher.

"Time for bed," my mom says, but I get her to give me five more minutes.

I want to finish my picture before I forget.